SHREDDERMAN

ATTACK *of the* TAGGER

by: WENDELIN VAN DRAANEN

ILLUSTRATED BY: BRIAN BIGGS

A YEARLING BOOK

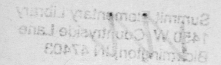
Published by Yearling, an imprint of Random House Children's Books
a division of Random House, Inc., New York

Visit us on the Web! www.randomhouse.com/kids and www.shredderman.com

Educators and librarians, for a variety of teaching tools, visit us at
www.randomhouse.com/teachers

ISBN-13: 978-0-440-41913-6
ISBN-10: 0-440-41913-1

Reprinted by arrangement with Alfred A. Knopf Books for Young Readers

Printed in the United States of America

May 2006

10 9 8 7 6

OPM

WENDELIN VAN DRAANEN

For Connor,
who shreds on his own and as a sidekick

BRIAN BIGGS

For Wilson and Elliot,
my very own nerds

CONTENTS

SHREDDERMAN

CHAPTER 1
Shreddin' Sidekick

My name's Nolan Byrd, but I have another name, too. A secret name.

Shredderman!

Everyone at school has been to *shredderman.com*, but no one knows that Shredderman is me. And maybe a lot of kids at school call me Nerd, but Shredderman they call cool.

Okay, not *every*one thinks Shredderman is cool. Alvin "Bubba" Bixby *hates* Shredderman.

Bubba's the reason I built the Shredderman Web site. He's a big bully with killer breath and rocky knuckles. Bubba used to flip over lunch trays.

Steal stuff!

Pound money out of little kids!

1

And since Bubba's sly—and a really good liar—no one could ever prove anything.

Enter Shredderman!

I converted my backpack into a spy-pack.

I hid my digital camera inside it!

And I started catching Bubba in the act—on camera!

Which is how Bubba's Big Butt—and a lot of his other dirty deeds—got posted on the Web for the whole world to see.

Serves him right for underestimating underdogs!

And it sure got teachers—and even Dr. Voss, our principal—to watch Bubba's every move. Cedar Valley Elementary is a much safer place since Shredderman came to town!

There *is* one person who knows that I'm Shredderman.

My sidekick.

My sidekick isn't younger than me.

Or smaller than me.

Or *weaker* than me.

Actually, he's got a lot more power than I do.

He's my...*shhhh*...teacher!

Everyone calls Mr. Green a hippie because he has long hair and drives an old Volkswagen van with dolphins painted all over it.

Mr. Green also plays the guitar. He loves his guitar! He plays it like crazy for music and then for all sorts of other reasons during the day.

He "punctuates" his points.

"Interludes" his lessons.

"Segues" his subjects.

"Crescendos" his comments.

What he really does is make tons of noise! Man, you should see his fingers fly! When Mr. Green plays, even Bubba Bixby listens.

People may make fun of Mr. Green and call him the Happy Hippie, but I think he's the coolest teacher ever. He's funny and smart and nice. And while everyone else may think I'm nerdy or geeky or dweeby, Mr. Green thinks I shred.

Which is what gave me the idea—and the courage—to become a secret cyber-superhero.

Everything was going great, too! Shredderman had exposed Bubba for the bully he is and no one had a clue that *I* was Shredderman. Not even my mom or dad! Well, Mr. Green figured it out, but instead of turning me over to Dr. Voss, he begged to be my sidekick.

"I'm going to be the best sidekick ever, Nolan!" he said.

"But, Mr. Green..." It seemed too weird. Like I should be *his* sidekick.

"And I've come up with a great name, too!"

"A name?"

"Yeah! The Bouncer!"

"The Bouncer?" I asked him. "Why the Bouncer?"

"Don't mess with Shredderman, man, or the Bouncer'll getcha!"

"Oh," I said, trying to picture it. "So what do you look like? A big ball?"

"No, man!" he laughed. "I look like a bouncer! Like one of those big cats that stands at the door to keep troublemakers out? Big muscles. Thick neck. Like a pro wrestler with tattoos."

"The Bouncer has *tattoos*?"

He shook his head. "Skip the tattoos. But you've got the idea, right?"

"Right."

"You'd better draw me with short hair." He snapped his fingers. "Hey, why don't you make me bald all over." He grinned. "No one'll ever suspect it's me!"

I went with the strong urge to rub my chin. "But why does Shredderman need a bouncer? He's Shredderman!"

He leaned in close and whispered, "*You* need a bouncer, Nolan, and I'm your man."

I shrugged. "Whatever you say, Mr. Green."

"Hey! What if I come up with a theme song?"

"A theme song? But that'll give away that it's you, won't it?"

"Nah...I'll write something electric. Distort it...pitch-shift it...add special effects....

I promise—it'll be outtasight!" He eyed me. "You *can* load song clips on your computer, can't you?"

"Uh-huh..."

"So let me see what I can do. You're the boss, though. If you don't dig it, I'll trash the idea." He grinned at me. "Or write something better."

So that's how I got myself a sidekick.

And a theme song.

The song's only about fifteen seconds when you boot up *shredderman.com*, but I like it.

It shreds.

Mr. Green has also helped me do new things with the site. It used to be "All Bubba, All the Time," but now it's got other stuff, too. Like a new Mystery Student every week, and joke contests, and riddles, and crossword puzzles. I keep Bubba's Big Butt posted for insurance, and I told Bubba in a Shredderman e-mail that it stays there until he starts being *nice* to people.

Shredderman also gets e-mails from kids

wanting me to add a joke to the *Jokes* link, or just asking, Who ARE you? Sometimes I even get messages from kids who want Shredderman to watch out for someone that's causing them trouble at school. Usually girls do this, which can get a little embarrassing.

They always sign off, LOVE.

So for a while everything was going great. Only kids from school knew about the site, which was fine with me. It kept me plenty busy, and besides, I didn't *want* all of Cedar Valley wondering who Shredderman was.

But then something happened. Something that cried out, "Shredderman, we need your help!" And in the name of truth and justice I couldn't just stand by and watch.

I had to *do* something!

CHAPTER 2
Toasting Peanut Butter

My dad's a reporter for the *Cedar Valley Gazette*. He works every day, even when he's not supposed to. He has a cubicle at the *Gazette* with pictures of me tacked up everywhere and a bubble gum dispenser that only costs a penny.

My mom writes missile-tracking software. She's got a computer at home and another one at Tech-Key, the company she works for. She works both places so she can be home when I am, since I've got no brothers or sisters or even a hamster to keep an eye on me.

I tell her I'm halfway through the fifth grade and can take care of myself, but she doesn't believe me. She always says the same thing: "You're not old enough, Nolan."

Sheez. Just what every superhero wants to hear.

But one Monday morning, Mom was all stressed out about a project deadline at work, so I said, "Don't worry about getting home for me, Mom. I can take care of myself after school."

"Nolan, you're not old enough."

"Mo-om! I am too!"

"No." She was packing my lunch, but she kept dropping things on the floor. First the baggies, then a knife, then the box of plastic spoons.

I handed the stuff up to her, saying, "I'll come straight home, do my homework, watch *The Gecko and Sticky*. . . . Everything'll be fine."

"I don't know, Nolan. . . ."

Wow! Something other than "no"! I jumped up and said, "I can take care of myself, Mom. Let me prove it!"

She shot a worried look at the clock. "Start by proving you can make your own breakfast while I clean this up."

"Sure!" I started zooming around the kitchen.

Eggos out of the freezer—check!

Peanut butter out of the cupboard—check!

Butter knife out of the drawer—check!

I smeared peanut butter all over two Eggos. I *love* peanut butter, and especially on waffles.

Yum!

Eggos in the toaster—check!

Toaster on medium—check!

Toaster lever down—check!

"Nolan? *Nolan?*"

"Yes, Mom?" I was getting down a plate.

"Nolan!" she screamed as she yanked up the toaster lever. Eggos went flying. She grabbed them out of the air. "Nolan Byrd, how many times have you seen me make waffles?"

"Uh...a lot?"

"Hundreds?"

"Probably," I agreed.

"*Thousands?*"

"Thousands?" I asked. "No...thousands means you would have made me Eggos every day for a minimum of five-point-four...five-point-four-eight years, and I don't think—"

"Nolan!" She wagged my waffles at me. "Have you *ever* seen me put the peanut butter on *before* I toasted them?"

I think those waffles would've come zinging at me like peanut butter Frisbees if Dad hadn't come into the kitchen. "Good morning!" he said, then checked us both over. "Uh-oh."

"Uh-oh is right!" Mom said.

"Take a deep breath, Eve," my dad said to her. "A deep, *deep* breath." He took the waffles from her and inspected them. "Peanut butter on, waffles frozen. Hmmmm." He turned to me. "Trying to make your own breakfast this morning, Nolan?"

I nodded.

Mom was taking deep breaths, but it wasn't helping much. "He's trying to show me that he can take care of himself."

Dad pulled two new waffles from the Eggo box and said to me, "Toast first, champ. Butter later. Otherwise the peanut butter melts and drips in the toaster and makes a stinky mess."

"Or starts a fire," Mom added.

Dad held the new waffles out to me. "Try it again."

So I did. And I didn't ruin the toaster. Didn't burn down the house. The waffles came up a perfect golden brown.

Dad seemed to be fine—he even microwaved the first two waffles and gobbled them up—but Mom barely ate anything and didn't say a word.

Then Dad's pager went off. He checked the number and said, "That's Mr. Zilch," and got up to call him back.

Mom sighed, then sighed again and looked at me.

"I'm sorry, Mom," I said.

She touched my cheek with her hand and said, "I just worry, honey. You are so smart, but sometimes I'm afraid you're living in your own world."

"But, Mom, it was just a little mistake!"

She sighed some more, and then Dad came back, saying, "Looks like I'll be doing a piece on graffiti."

Mom turned to him. "Graffiti? In Cedar Valley?"

"Some hotshot sprayed red paint all over the shops in Old Town Square."

"Gang graffiti?"

"No. Apparently it's some childish picture and a long line of red paint."

"How are you going to make a story about a long line of red paint?" I asked him.

Dad shrugged. "I'll interview the shop owners— I'm sure they'll give me a lot to work with." He looked from me to Mom and said, "We okay here?"

She nodded. "Of course. We just take it one little step at a time." She gave me a worried smile. "Right, honey?"

I was dying to say, I'm not a baby, Mom! Maybe I don't know how to make my own breakfast. Maybe I button things wrong or tie them backward. Maybe I miss whole conversations because I'm thinking about something else. But under all that, I'm Shredderman! I've saved Cedar Valley Elementary from the evils of Bubba Bixby! I'm strong and I'm smart and I'm brave! I'm a cyber-superhero!

What's toasting an Eggo compared to the fight for truth and justice?

But I couldn't tell her. It's against the Superhero Rules to give away your secret identity. It must be. That's why they call it a *secret* identity.

So I just tried to smile back and said, "Toast first. Butter later."

She gave me a kiss on my superhero forehead. "That's my boy."

I wiped it off, then heard the morning bell ring across the street. School was open! Morning recess had begun!

I zoomed down to my bathroom.

I brushed my teeth!

I zoomed up to my bedroom.

I grabbed my backpack!

I zoomed to the kitchen.

I snagged my lunch!

I zoomed out the front door, calling, "Love you, Mom!"

"Love you, too, honey!" Mom called back. "See you after school!"

But the minute I zoomed onto campus, I could tell that something was wrong.

And what it was turned out to be a whole lot worse than toasted peanut butter.

CHAPTER 3
Du-uh!

From clear across the blacktop I could see that my teacher was not being the Happy Hippie—he was madder than the Green Hornet. He was storming toward the teachers' parking lot, surrounded by kids.

I caught up and asked, "What's wrong, Mr. Green?" because I'd never seen him mad before. Testy, sure. Or annoyed. Or even a little grumpy.

But mad?

Not Mr. Green.

"I cannot believe it!" he said, marching along the blacktop. He had a rag in one hand, a bottle of clear liquid in the other.

"Believe what?" I asked. "What happened?"

Mr. Green didn't answer me, but all of a sudden he stopped and turned around and said to everyone, "This is not cool. And you can tell whoever did it, they won't get away with it!" Then he started marching again, straight for his van.

I was next to Ryan Voss, so I asked, "What did they do?" I figured he *had* to know—not only is he a sixth grader, he's the principal's son and knows everything.

"Beats me," he said.

"Dude, didn't you hear?" Carl Blanco said to me. "Someone tagged the Green Machine!"

I said, "Tagged Mr. Green's van? What do you mean?"

Carl pulled a face at me. "Not like the *game*, Nerd. They tagged it with spray paint."

"Seriously?" Ryan asked.

Carl nodded. "I heard it's bright red."

"Red?" I stopped walking. The same color as the graffiti in Old Town!

Wow.

I shifted into my power-walk and caught up to Mr. Green. But he didn't want to hear about my dad's assignment for the *Gazette*. He just wanted to get to his van.

When we got there, Nica Parker said, "Oh, that's awful!" and it was. Someone had spray-painted a great big dumb-baby face right over Mr. Green's dolphins. Red circle. Red eyes rolling up. Red buckteeth going left and right.

And coming out of the giant dumb-baby mouth was a talkie balloon with a great big red *Du-uh!* inside it.

Mr. Green wet his rag and started scrubbing.

Everyone crowded around.

The paint didn't budge.

Then the warning bell rang and Mr. Green said, "Get to class! All of you. Shoo!"

No one moved. We just kept watching him scrub.

"Now!" he shouted. "Go to class or you'll be tardy!"

"Du-uh!" someone from the left side said.

Mr. Green froze mid-swipe. Everyone held their breath. Eyeballs went boinging all around.

Mine spotted Carl, smirking. And some other sixth graders around him were smirking, too. Like Ryan Voss. And Brad Waxton. And Richie Hatini.

"Who said that?" Mr. Green asked.

No one breathed a molecule.

"Who *said* that?" He stood straight up. "So. You're a vandal *and* a coward, huh?"

"*Braaawk-brawk-brawk,*" came a voice from the other side of the crowd.

Everyone turned.

But before we could figure out who'd made the chicken sound, Dr. Voss appeared, her voice cracking like a whip. "Children! Get to class. You'll all be tardy!"

Everyone charged out of there. Everyone but

me. I ducked behind the back bumper of Mr. Green's van and waited.

When Dr. Voss got over to Mr. Green, she said, "I understand you're upset about this, Elmo, but there's no reason to make a school-wide spectacle of it."

Elmo? My teacher's name was *Elmo*?

Wait. The *Bouncer's* name was Elmo?

I fell flat on my butt.

Mr. Green was saying, "Someone did it this morning. Right here, in the parking lot."

I peeked around the back of Mr. Green's van. Dr. Voss was giving the dumb-baby a stern look. "We'll see what we can do."

She started to walk off, but Mr. Green stopped her. "Exactly what does that mean *this* time, Ivana?"

"That we'll . . . look into it," Dr. Voss said.

"*How* will we be looking into it?" Mr. Green asked her.

She frowned at him. "Let me give that some thought, will you?"

Mr. Green said, "How about we start by calling the police. Then let's ask Dusty to look through the trash bins for the spray can."

She put her fists on her hips. "Our custodian was not hired to dig through trash."

Mr. Green shook his head. "Fine. Then I'll do it."

"You have a class to run."

"Okay...I'll get my class to help me, then."

"Voluntarily?"

He shrugged. "Sure."

She nodded. "That shouldn't anger any parents. But make them wash up afterward. And don't take too much time away from class!"

"Wait!" he called after her. "Can you ask the teachers to look through backpacks?"

"Well, I don't know about *that*." Her frown was back. "It could've been anyone. They could've just walked through the field here, up the hill. They could've—"

"Could you *please* just ask the other teachers to check? My mural is ruined! It has a lot of sentimental value to me."

"I'm sure it does," Dr. Voss said with a smirk, then turned her back and headed for the office. "We'll do the best we can!" she called over her shoulder. "In the meantime, I can see your class lined up outside your room!"

When she was gone, I popped up from behind the bumper and said, "Don't worry, Mr. Green. Whoever did it, we'll catch 'em!"

"Nolan! Where'd you come from?"

"Back there," I said, pointing to where I'd been.

"Did you hear . . . everything?"

"Uh-huh. And if Dr. Voss won't help you, I will."

CHAPTER 4
Toilet Bowl Spy

I don't think Mr. Green believed I could help him. He wouldn't even talk about it. He just wanted to scour the school. He wanted to call the police. He wanted to do things *his* way.

His way?

Sheez. Some sidekick.

So I ran one way around campus to get into line with the rest of my class while Mr. Green walked a different way.

You can't be too careful when your secret identities are at stake!

Mr. Green didn't say a word to any of us when he unlocked the classroom. He just propped open the door and inspected backpacks and hands as we went inside.

Since I was the last in line, I kept an eagle eye on everyone in front of me. Especially Bubba Bixby and *his* sidekicks, Kevin and Max. They whispered and laughed a lot, but Mr. Green couldn't find a thing on them. He looked hard, too.

That didn't mean they *hadn't* done the dumb-baby face, but it did mean they thought they wouldn't get caught.

Villains are sly at covering their tracks.

When we were all seated, Mr. Green didn't pick up his guitar and strum through "Good Day Sunshine" or any of his other good-morning songs. He just stood in front of the class with his arms crossed, frowning.

Finally he said, "You know why we had that little inspection this morning, right?"

Everyone nodded.

"Does anyone want to volunteer any information about what happened to my van?"

No one said a word.

Mr. Green sighed. "Well, if you change your mind, you can always leave an anonymous note on my desk." Then he said, "Does anyone want to help me dig through trash cans for evidence?"

"Sure!" a lot of us said.

"Raise your hand if you're willing to look around campus for a can of red spray paint."

Everyone's hand went up.

Even Bubba's.

"Okay, then." He looked at his watch. "Here are the rules: No noise. No going into other classrooms. And don't even *think* about stepping a toe off campus."

Everyone nodded.

"If you find the spray can, do *not* touch it! Get me, and I'll pick it up with a rag. We don't want to mess up fingerprints." He yanked open his desk and pulled out a whistle. "When you hear this blow, you've got thirty seconds to get back to class. We all clear on the rules?"

Everyone agreed.

"Anyone *not* want to do this? Raise your hand now; this is strictly voluntary."

All hands stayed down.

He told different tables what part of school he wanted them to scour, then said, "Let's go."

I slipped my digital camera out of its secret compartment in my backpack and put it in my sweatshirt pocket.

Just in case.

Then I filed out with the rest of the kids, only I didn't start looking in the area I was supposed to look. Instead, I zoomed around behind our classroom, behind the computer lab, over to the boys'

29

bathroom where Bubba holds his meetings.

His bully-club meetings.

I checked over both shoulders, then ducked inside the bathroom and looked around.

Nobody home.

So I zoomed down to the last stall, closed the door, and stood on the toilet seat.

No shoes showing!

I clamped down tight on my camera.

Didn't want it to fall in!

And I was barely in position when, sure enough, Bubba, Max, and Kevin came busting into the bathroom.

I couldn't see them, but believe me—I'd recognize their voices anywhere. Max's is kind of whiny, Kevin always sounds like he has a cold, and Bubba, well, if you've ever been face to face with Bubba-breath, it's something you'll never forget.

Max was busting up, "Hee hee hee!"

Kevin was going, "Ha ha ha," through his nose.

Then Bubba said, "Is the Happy Hippie bent or what? Dude! His beak is totally tweaked!"

"He totally thinks it's you, dude," Max said. "Did you see the way he was checking you over for red paint?"

"I hope he accuses me, man. I'll sue!"

Max said, "So *now* are you gonna tell us? Huh huh huh?"

"Shut up, stupid," Bubba said. "You sound like a dumb-baby."

"Like that dumb-baby on the Green Machine, duuuu-uh!" Kevin said.

"So do you, stupid!" Bubba told Kevin. "Which is why I'm not breathin' a word to either of you."

"Come on, dude," Max whined. "It's *us*."

"Yeah, we're not gonna squeal!" Kevin said.

My ear pushed out even harder. So it wasn't Bubba after all? Then I heard Bubba say, "I'll tell you this much—you know him."

"Who, man, who?" Kevin asked.

Max said, "Do you think they'll nail him?"

"I ain't squealin'," Bubba said. "But believe me—they'll never nail him. The dude is, like, invincible."

All of a sudden, sunlight came streaming into the bathroom and I heard Mr. Green's voice say, "Gentlemen, this is not a potty party."

"'Course not, Mr. Green!" Bubba said. "We're just checking out all the trash cans in here. Someone could've stuck it way down under all these paper towels or something."

I could hear Mr. Green shuffling around for a minute. Then he said, "Get out there, boys. And make yourselves useful or line up in front of the classroom."

"Yes, sir!" they said.

When they were all gone and I was sure the coast was clear, I hopped off the toilet and snuck out of the bathroom.

So they thought the guy who tagged Mr. Green's van was invincible, huh?

We'd see about that.

I'd find out who he was!

I'd teach him to mess with my sidekick!

This was a job for Shredderman!

CHAPTER 5
The Can Turns Up

At Cedar Valley Elementary, the kindergartners hang their backpacks on a big wooden rack outside their classroom. It's in a little alcove, and when I was in kindergarten, I never worried about anyone stealing my stuff.

That was before Bubba Bixby came to town.

I also never worried about anyone putting criminal evidence in my backpack, but that's exactly what happened to Trinity's little sister. When the A.M. kindergartners were packing up to go home, she found the red spray can. It was stashed in her backpack.

Trinity sits across from me in Mr. Green's class.

Trinity, Freddy, Randy, and I are all assigned to Table 4. Freddy and Randy are just regular guys. Not bullies, just medium mean. Trinity, though, is pretty nice. She's not very good at math, but she can draw like crazy. Especially horses. She's great at drawing horses.

By the time we got in from lunch, everyone had heard about the spray can turning up. The police had been there taking pictures, talking to Mr. Green and Dr. Voss, walking around with the spray can in a big plastic bag.

Trinity was pretty worked up about it, too, because the can was found in her sister's backpack. "Who could have put it there?" she whispered across the table to me.

"*She* put it there, Pony-girl," Randy said.

"Did not!"

"Sure she did. She drew a picture of herself on Mr. Green's van!" He rolled his eyes up and pulled a dumb-baby face. "Du-uh."

Trinity said, "Shut up, Randy. I wasn't asking you."

He shrugged and gave Freddy an evil grin. Then he looked back at her and said, "Sorry. I just didn't hear your *boyfriend* answering you."

Boyfriend? My eyes got big. My cheeks turned red. Was he talking about *me*?

"Shut up, stupid," Trinity told him. "He's not my boyfriend." She looked at me. "He's just my friend." She whipped around to face Freddy and Randy. "Which is more than I can say about you guys."

Then the three of them pulled faces and stuck tongues out at each other and said, "Shut up," "No, you shut up," about twenty times back and forth.

I just sat there feeling embarrassed.

Now, all day I'd been trying to figure out how I could get back to Mr. Green's van without someone seeing me. But before lunch Mr. Green was

in such a bad mood that I didn't want to ask him anything. Then at recess and lunch there were too many people around. Including police!

It would have been easy to get back to his van if I didn't have to do it without being seen. But being invisible was key. The power of

Shredderman was in people *not* knowing who he was. In people thinking Shredderman could be anyone.

After lunch Mr. Green wasn't quite so mad. So when our class was on the way over to computer lab, I asked him, "Can I go do something? I'll be right back."

He started to ask me what I was going to do, but I could see him change his mind. Instead, he gave me a quick nod and said, "Hurry back."

To get to the teachers' parking lot, you've either got to go through the playground or past the office. If you go through the playground, you're wide open. Anyone in the portable classrooms might spot you.

But if you go past the office, well, that's where Dr. Voss is. And getting spotted by her would be worse than getting spotted by all the other teachers combined! But still. There was one principal and about twenty-five teachers. Going by the office might be more dangerous, but the odds were definitely better.

So I broke off from my class on the way to the computer lab and ran behind the portables, behind the library, behind the multi-purpose room, all the way to the office.

I ducked behind a bush and could see the office lady, Mrs. Holler, through the window. She was on the phone, leaning on an elbow, looking out at the flowers in the courtyard.

The minute she turned her back, I zoomed across the courtyard and dove behind the hedge that runs next to the office building.

I crawled on my hands and knees past the office and under Dr. Voss's window. I crawled, crawled, crawled, clear to the back of the building.

There was a barricade of about twenty big green plastic sacks full of yard waste, but on the other side—oh, yeah! The parking lot!

The teachers' parking lot is like a V with cars

along both edges. One side is by the office, the other is by a cliff of bushes that drops down to the soccer fields. I had to get from where I was to the other side. To the cliff side.

I looked left. Nobody around.

I looked right. The coast was clear!

I crawled along a couple of car bumpers, then scooted between a pickup truck and a fancy silver car with spoked wheels.

And I was getting ready to jet across to the other side of the parking lot when *vroom!* The silver car right next to me started up!

I crawled around the pickup truck and watched the fancy car back out. My heart was pounding like crazy. Had they seen me?

No! I told myself. They wouldn't back away if they knew I was practically under the wheel! They'd get out and ask me why I was sneaking around the parking lot. They'd ... And then I saw who was driving away in that fancy silver car.

Dr. Voss!

I'd almost been run over by the principal!

I watched her drive off, then made myself calm down a little. I didn't have time to waste being scared! I had a picture to take, and I had to do it fast!

So I hurried across the parking lot and captured Dumb-Baby digitally, then I snuck back the way I'd come.

And now I couldn't *wait* for school to let out so I could get to work on the next step of my plan!

CHAPTER 6
Old Town

"Wow, honey," Mom said as I blasted through the front door. "What happened?"

"What do you mean?" I asked, peeling off my backpack.

"You're so dirty!" She started picking stuff off the back of my shirt and out of my hair. "You've got leaves, and prickers, and . . . Nolan, your jeans are filthy!"

I shook her off but noticed she was right—the knees of my jeans were caked with dirt.

"Alvin Bixby didn't push you down again, did he? Because if he did—"

"No, Mom! I had a great day!"

"You . . . you did?"

"Uh-huh."

"Looks like you got some . . . exercise today. No computer lab at recess?"

I got myself a juice box from the fridge. "Nope."

She smiled. "Great! So . . . who'd you play with?"

I shrugged. "Just played." I vacuumed up juice fast. "And you know what?"

"What?"

"Now I want to go ride my bike."

She blinked at me. "Really?"

I grabbed another juice box. "Uh-huh. You're right. I *should* get more exercise."

She was blinking like crazy. "Well, okay...! You remember the rules of the road?"

"Of course!"

"Wear your helmet, ride on the right side, look both ways before you—"

"Mo-om!"

"Okay, okay! Sorry, honey."

I slurped out the bottom of the juice box, tossed it in the trash, and headed for the garage.

"Why are you taking your backpack, Nolan?"

"Uh...in case I find something cool on my ride."

"But...aren't all those books heavy?"

I dumped the books and said, "I feel like going for a loooooong ride, so don't worry, okay, Mom?"

"But—"

"Mo-om! I'll be fine!"

She scrambled around, then handed me her cell phone. "Here. Take this. In case you get a flat or something."

I rolled my eyes. A superhero calling his mom to the rescue. Sheez.

I'd been to Old Town Square a bunch of times before, but never on my bike, and never alone. It was about ten minutes away in the car, I knew that, so I figured it would take me about fifteen on my bike. I may not be great at basketball or soccer, but I can *fly* on my bike. I blasted down the street. My digital speedometer said 10, 15, 20, 24.5 miles per hour! I was passing people!

Dogs!

Cars!

By the time I got to Old Town Square, I swear there was a superhero cape flapping in the wind behind me.

You can't drive through Old Town Square. You have to park outside and walk. And that goes for bikes and skateboards and scooters, too. There's a nice green park in the middle, with benches and trees and squirrels and statues. And all the stores are connected in a great big U around three sides of the park.

The stores all look the same. They're built out of wood and have a nonstop porch going from

one to the next to the next. The boards always creak when you walk, which I hate the sound of, but Mom says it's part of the Old Town charm.

But before I even got inside the square, I saw what I was looking for.

Red paint.

And right away I could tell that it *had* been done by the same person who'd sprayed Mr. Green's van. On the side of the building, right where everyone could see it when they walked into the square, was a giant dumb-baby.

Eyes rolling up.

Buckteeth going left and right.

And a talkie balloon that said, *Du-uh!*

I locked my bike, took out my digital camera, and moved in.

There were people all over the place, so I just tried to act like I was one of them as I found a place to get a good picture. And after walking back and forth about ten times I figured it didn't really matter if someone saw me taking pictures. Who knew me around here, anyway?

So I just went up, clicked a few shots, and hurried back to my bike. But while I was unlocking my bike, a whole bunch of *other* kids came skidding up to the bike rack next to mine. They were wearing backpacks, too, and helmets. And normally it wouldn't have made me nervous or anything, but the way they were laughing made me feel a little self-conscious.

Usually when I hear people laughing kind of mean like that, they're laughing at *me*.

So I looked down and retied my shoe, hoping they'd go away and leave me alone.

Then one of them said, "Du-uh!"

Du-uh?

I peeked at them through the spokes of my front wheel. They weren't even looking at me! They were looking at the graffiti.

One by one, all five of them peeled off their helmets.

These were boys from school!

I ducked lower, trying to hide behind my bike. Two of them I knew were sixth graders, but I didn't know their names. The two other sixth graders I did know—Carl Blanco and Ryan Voss. And the last boy was big enough to be a sixth grader but was only in fifth grade.

Bubba Bixby.

They started walking. And I started trailing them! I hid behind a trash can. A bench. A tree. I scooted from one to the next to the next,

following the five of them toward the red dumb-baby.

When they finally stood still, I aimed my camera between the slats of a bench and *bzzzzz, click! Bzzzzz, click! Bzzzzz, click!* I got pictures of them laughing. Of them giving each other high-fives and low-fives. I got lots of pictures! And the minute they took off to walk through Old Town, I took off for home.

Shredderman had work to do!

CHAPTER 7
Fighting Back

I rode home even faster than I'd ridden there. *Pump, pump, pump,* I was cranking those pedals! Maximizing those gear ratios! I even hopped a curb for the first time in my life.

Wa-hoo!

When I came in through the garage, Mom acted like I'd just come home from war. "Where have you been? What took you so long? I kept looking out the window but didn't see you go by once!"

"Mo-om!"

"Don't Mo-om me!" She followed me to the fridge. "Honey, what's gotten *into* you?"

I slurped another juice box dry. Didn't even close the fridge.

"Honey?" She took off my helmet. "You're sweating!"

Hmmm. Did superheroes sweat? Not that I'd ever seen....

I swatted her off. "Mo-om! I just went riding, okay? Quit making such a big deal out of it." I jabbed a straw through the next juice box and headed down to my room. "Gotta do my homework," I told her. "And there's a ton of it!"

She just stood there, blinking.

I put up my *Shhhhh! Concentrating!* sign, closed the door tight, and got to work.

Digital camera connected to USB port—check!

Images loaded—check!

Images displayed—check!

I zoomed in on the two sixth graders I didn't know, then got my yearbook down.

At first I just sat there with my yearbook on my lap. Of all the books in the world, this was the only one I hated. Not because of my picture—it was just as good as anyone else's, and a whole lot better than Ian McCoy's! His eyes were half closed and he looked like he was about to sneeze.

But my fourth-grade teacher, Mrs. Ankmeyer, had let us have a signing party where we all got to sign each other's yearbooks. And while I was writing stuff like "Have a cool summer" and "Remember: $E=mc^2$—you'll need it in 5th grade!" and "I hope we're friends next year," some kids were writing nerd jokes in mine:

"You're so nerdy, you'd probably trip on a cordless phone!"

"You're so nerdy, you'd bring a spoon to the Super Bowl!"

"You're so nerdy, if you threw a rock at the ground, you'd miss!"

I actually cried when I got home. Why did they have to be mean like that? Did they really think it was funny? Why didn't anybody *like* me?

Mom wanted to talk to Mrs. Ankmeyer about it, but I told her not to. It was embarrassing enough without her making a big deal out of it. I just put the yearbook away and tried to forget about it.

Of course all that happened before I became a cyber-superhero. And now that I was, well, super-heroes don't cry.

They fight back.

I opened up the yearbook and started flipping through the pages. All four of the sixth graders I'd seen in Old Town had been in Mr. Green's fifth-grade class last year. There was Ryan Voss, Carl

Blanco, Manny Davis, and A. J. Penne. They all looked nice. Like they could be anybody's friend.

Even mine.

Then I remembered: *Bubba* was hanging around with them. Scratch that friend idea!

But what was Ryan Voss doing with *Bubba*? He was the principal's son! The sixth-grade class president! He was really popular! Did his mom know he was riding around town with Bubba? And why did Bubba get to ride with a bunch of sixth graders, anyway? Were they afraid of what he might do if they *didn't* let him hang around with them? Was he blackmailing them into being in the group?

I scanned the yearbook pictures of Ryan, Carl, Manny, and A.J. into the computer, then downloaded the pictures I'd taken at Old Town.

Then I just sat there, thinking. I felt like I had a Super Soaker filled to the brim but didn't really know where to start spraying. What I had so far didn't prove *anything*. So Bubba had bragged to Max and Kevin that he knew who the Tagger was.

Bubba lied like crazy!

So Bubba had been at Old Town with a bunch of sixth graders slapping around high-fives. So what?

Maybe they just thought the dumb-baby was funny.

Or maybe they just didn't like Mr. Green.

"No-lan! Din-ner!" my mom called up the hallway.

I saved everything quick, then clicked off my monitor in the nick of time. "Nolan?" Dad was peeking in my room. "Hey, champ, it's dinnertime."

"Coming!" I tripped all over myself getting out of the room before he could wander in. "How'd work go?" I asked, then led the way to the kitchen. "Did they find out who sprayed the graffiti?"

"Not yet," Dad said. "But the Tagger's been busy. I suppose you know that he sprayed your teacher's van?"

"The Tagger?" Mom asked, putting a platter of chicken on the table. "Is that what they're calling him?"

"That's right," my dad said as we all scooted up in our chairs. "My headline tomorrow reads: TAGGER HITS OLD TOWN. But he's hit two other places now, too."

"*Two* other?" I asked, grabbing a chicken leg.

"Mr. Green's van, and the Cedar Creek Bridge."

I was paying attention, boy! I asked, "All dumb-babies?"

"Uh-huh."

"Wait a minute," Mom said, serving me carrots. "Dumb-babies? What do you mean? Did they say anything?"

I pulled a dumb-baby face. "Du-uh!"

"Nolan!" she scolded.

Dad laughed. "'Du-uh' is exactly what they all say, Eve. And that's pretty much what they *look* like."

I chomped down on my chicken, ripping meat off the bone like a caveman. "Were they all red, Dad?"

"The one on the bridge is purple."

I was gobbling food like mad! "They don't have *any* idea who did it?"

"Just some punk kid causing trouble, I'm sure. The police are on top of it, but they don't have much to go on. They've started questioning places that sell spray paint, but that'll take some time." He looked at me and said, "Good grief, Nolan, slow down!"

"Milk, please!" I said through my chicken. "More carrots, too!"

Superheroes need strong bones. And good night vision!

Dinner was barely over when Dad got a call. And when he hung up, he grabbed his coat and said, "The Tagger struck again. I'm going to go check it out."

"But, Steven!" my mom said, then threw her hands in the air. There was no sense arguing with him, and she knew it.

"Can I come?" I asked.

"I thought you had a mountain of homework," Mom said.

"I do, but I'll get it done!"

Dad said to my mom, "I think it's great that he's showing interest. It'd be fun to have him along."

Mom shrugged. "Okay."

"Yes!" I cried, then raced down to my room to collect my Shredderman gear.

CHAPTER 8
Along for the Ride

The police were still there when we got to the toddler park where the Tagger had been. It was a little neighborhood park with two swings, a tube slide, a giant tic-tac-toe game, and a big ship with about ten steering wheels.

And now it also had a whole family of dumb-baby faces. They were sprayed on a tall fence that was between the park and some houses.

The police had some big floodlights lighting up the night. And all those dumb-baby faces looked kind of creepy. The paint went from one to the other to the other. It looked like a string of big purple ghosts with buckteeth!

"What a moron," one of the policemen was

saying. He was shaking his head good. "What's the deal with the 'du-uh'? Is he saying *he's* dumb?"

Dad shook his head, too. "I think he's saying he thinks whatever he's spraying is dumb."

The policeman snorted. "Well, he's sure got that backward."

Another policeman came over and shook hands with my dad. "Glad you could make it, Steven."

"Thanks for the call." Dad pulled me in by the shoulder and said, "This is my son, Nolan. Nolan, this is Sergeant Klubb." He looked at me and added, "You've heard me talk about my friend Sarge, right? Well, this is him."

Sergeant Klubb gave me a crooked smile and

said, "So you're Nolan. . . . I've heard tales about you, too. Can you really count by nine and a halfs?"

"Da-ad!" I said, and turned redder than the dumb-baby on Mr. Green's van.

Dad ruffled my hair and said, "Sorry, champ." Then he nodded at the purple dumb-babies and

said to Sarge, "It's too late to make the morning paper, but we'll get it in Wednesday's. Any leads?"

"No witnesses so far. No help from the stores yet, either. We'll catch him, though. I'm not putting up with this junk in Cedar Valley. They want to tag? Let 'em go to the city, where they call it art."

"Hey, Sarge!" a policeman called from inside the tube slide. "There's a slew of them in here!"

We followed him over and looked inside the slide. There were rolling eyes and buckteeth all over the place! And at the bottom a great big *Du-uh!*

Sarge was mad. "What a punk! Like he paid for this equipment?" The radio on his belt crackled. He pushed a button and said, "Klubb here."

A voice on the radio said, "We've got a five-ninety-four at five-twelve Highland."

"Copy that," he said. "In progress?"

"Negative," the voice on the radio answered.

"On my way," Sarge said, then turned to Dad. "Another tagging about five blocks away. Since it's too late for tomorrow's paper, how about I leave whatever turns up tonight on your voice mail?"

"Sounds good," Dad said. "I'll help out any way I can."

Sarge nodded. "See if you can't rally a community watch. That would really help nail this guy!"

When we got back in the car, Dad said, "So, what do you think?"

I scooted my backpack between my feet. I hadn't had the chance to take any pictures. Hadn't really had the chance to do *anything*. And what was the point in trying to help when the police were doing a fine job without me? They'd figure out who the Tagger was *way* before I could.

I felt kind of stupid. I'd thought I was a superhero.

Ha.

"Nolan?" Dad was driving but looking more at me than the road.

I shrugged. "I didn't know there were so many police in Cedar Valley."

He nodded.

"I also didn't know you were a policeman's helper." I looked at him. "It's pretty cool that you do that, Dad."

He smiled real big at me, and right then I wanted to tell him how I was trying to help, too. How I wasn't just a boy who fumbled and stumbled and tried to toast peanut butter. I was a cyber-superhero! And I'd been working the whole day on figuring out a way to trap the Tagger.

But I couldn't tell him. Mom and Dad were the last people who could know! They wouldn't understand why Bubba's Big Butt had to be on the World Wide Web. They would start worrying. Start making me *change* things.

It would be the end of Shredderman.

But... maybe I could help my dad and the police without giving away my secret identity.

"Dad?"

"Yes?"

"Off the record?"

"Sure...."

"There are four sixth graders at school I think you should have Sarge look into."

"There are?"

"Uh-huh." My heart was beating like crazy. "I, um...I heard some kids at school talking."

"You *did?* What did they say?"

"They were laughing about the dumb-baby and giving each other high-fives and stuff. From the way they were acting, I think it might be one of them."

"Hmmm." He glanced at me. "Why didn't you tell me this before?"

I shrugged. Then I said, "Don't tell anyone I told, okay?"

He eyed me. "I understand. You've got enough troubles at school without being labeled a rat, am I right?"

It seemed like a really good excuse, anyway. So I nodded and said, "Can you just say that you got an anonymous tip?"

"Sure. So who are they?"

"Carl Blanco, Manny Davis, A. J. Penne, and Ryan Voss."

He was writing like mad on his dashboard paper pad but stopped when I said Ryan's name. "Ryan Voss? Your principal's son?"

"Uh-huh."

He sort of frowned at me.

"I know, but he was with them."

He took a deep breath, held it, then wrote down Ryan's name as he let it out. "Anonymous tip, huh?"

"Yeah. Maybe say it was on your voice mail at work?"

"Okay. . . ." He snapped open his cell phone and punched in a number.

"Who are you calling?" I asked.

He had one eye on the road, the other on me. "Sarge. Might as well get this ball rolling tonight."

CHAPTER 9
Mapping Out Evidence

That night Dad came in after I was already in bed. He whispered, "You awake, Nolan?"

I sat up. "Did they catch him?"

"No...." He sat on the edge of my bed. "I'm afraid those names you gave me didn't turn up much."

"*Nothing?*"

He sighed. "Just some indignant parents."

"They were mad?"

He nodded. "Especially the Vosses."

I lay back down and hooked my big stuffed gecko in the crook of my arm. "Oh. Sorry."

"It's okay." He ruffled my hair. "Good night,

champ." He ruffled my gecko. "Good night, gecko monster."

"His name's Sticky, Dad, and he's not a monster!"

"I know that," he laughed. "Now get some sleep."

Sleep. Ha. He'd just riled my brain all up. Was I wrong about the sixth graders? I tried to remember everything Bubba had said in the bathroom. Had he just been talking big to show off to Max and Kevin? Or did he really know who had tagged Mr. Green's van?

Call it superhero sonar, I don't know. But by now I was clicked into Bubba and his evil ways. And I was pretty sure he *hadn't* just been talking big to Kevin and Max.

And so what if none of the sixth graders had helped the police—since when did villains volunteer information to the law? No, I still thought one of them was the Tagger.

But which one?

I started picturing all the places dumb-baby faces had shown up. I tried to put them together in a mental map, but I kept getting lost in my own head.

So I crept out of bed, turned on my computer, and dialed up the Internet.

Maps, click!

Enter address—I typed in our zip code—click!

A map of half the state appeared on the screen.

I zoomed in until it was just Cedar Valley.

I covered my printer with my comforter.

Shhh!

I clicked on Print and *wraaaaang, wraaaaang, wraaaaang, wraaaaang!*

It was still louder than anything!

I flipped off the monitor, grabbed the printout and my comforter, and jumped back in bed.

Nobody showed up.

So I got out of bed again, flicked on my flashlight, and started putting X's on the map. One where the school was, one on the bridge, one at Old Town Square, and one at the toddler park. Then I went back to the computer and typed in the address of the latest tagging that had come in on Sarge's radio—512 Highland. And when I knew where 512 Highland was, I added the last X to my printed map.

Hmmmmm.

If only I knew where those four sixth graders lived.

I cracked open my door and listened for noise from my parents' room.

Not a peep.

I tiptoed down to my mother's desk, found the phone book, and sneaked back to my room.

Shhhhhh!

I started looking up names. And pretty soon I figured out that I couldn't figure out a thing! I didn't know any of the sixth graders' parents' names. Except for Dr. Voss—hers was Ivana—but there weren't even any Vosses in the book!

So now what?

Maybe I could hack into the school's computer database and find out where they lived that way.

Or hey! Why didn't I just call my sidekick? He'd had all four of them in class before....

I dug through the Greens. There were lots of Greens living in Cedar Valley, but only one "E. Green."

I checked the clock. 10:45—way too late to call.

Unless, of course, you're a superhero, and then it's never too late to call your sidekick, right?

But how was I going to call without being heard? The phone on Mom's desk is a corded one. The portable one is in Mom and Dad's bedroom.

Then I remembered—I still had Mom's cell phone in my backpack!

I dug it up!

I flicked it open!

I punched in Mr. Green's number!

On the third ring, I realized what I was doing. Aaaargh! I was calling my teacher! At 10:49 at night! He was going to kill me!

Before I could hang up, someone answered, "Hello?" The voice didn't sound sleepy. It sounded jumpy.

"Uh...Elmo?" I said, just in case there was another "E. Green" living in Cedar Valley.

"What's that?" Then I guess it registered because he said, "Yeah. Who's this?"

"Shredderman," I whispered. "Sorry it's so late."

There was a moment of silence, then, "What's the square root of twenty-two thousand eight hundred one?"

"One fifty-one," I shot back.

"Well, hello, Shredderman," he said. "You take this pretty seriously, don't you?"

"Truth and justice are not to be taken lightly."

My voice sounded older. Deeper. Like it wasn't even me talking.

"True. So what's going on? Is everything all right?"

"I need some information." I buried my head under the comforter and whispered, "Don't ask a lot of questions— just help me if you can, okay? This has to do with your van."

"Go for it, Shredderman."

"I need addresses for Carl Blanco, Manny Davis, A. J. Penne, and Ryan Voss. They were all in your class last year."

"Ryan *Voss?*"

"Uh-huh."

"Hmmm," he said, and I could tell he was thinking about a dozen things at once. "Hold the line, okay? I've got last year's records in my file cabinet."

It took about five minutes, but when he finally picked up the phone again, he said, "Got 'em. Ready?"

"Yes!" I grabbed a pencil and scribbled down the addresses, then said, "Thanks!"

"I trust you'll use the information with respect. Giving it out puts me in touchy territory, you understand?"

"I understand." I hung up and got to work. One by one, I found the sixth graders' addresses on the Internet. One by one, I marked them on my map. When I was done, I could see that A. J. Penne and Manny Davis lived quite a ways away from

the places the graffiti had been sprayed. Especially from the purple dumb-babies that had shown up that night.

But Ryan Voss and Carl Blanco both lived nearby.

Could Ryan or Carl really be the Tagger?

I thought for a minute, then decided.

Helping the police hadn't done any good.

It was time to try it my way.

CHAPTER 10
Spraying Cyberspace!

I sat in front of my computer with dumb-baby images galore and some pretty good shots of Bubba, Carl, Manny, A.J., and Ryan giving high-fives in Old Town. But what should I *do* with them? I needed proof.

I needed to catch the Tagger in the act.

I scrolled through the pictures again and again. Then I noticed something. Something I'd been too nervous to pay attention to when I'd taken the shots.

I double-checked the pictures.

Sure enough, one boy was in all the high-five, low-five shots.

Four of the boys were *giving* high-fives.

Only one was taking.

Ryan Voss.

Then I remembered what Bubba had said to Max and Kevin in the bathroom: "The dude is, like, invincible."

Plus, from my map I knew that Ryan's was the house nearest the toddler park.

Evidence was mounting!

I blinked at the picture of him on my computer screen. Could it be? And if it was, how much trouble did I want to get into trying to trap the principal's son?

Nolan Byrd was nervous, but Shredderman was mad! Who cared about trouble! We needed truth! We needed justice!

Justice? All of a sudden, my brain had a dangerous thought.

And Shredderman loved it!

Oh, yeah! That'd be justice, all right! Poetic

justice! But I had to set it up just right. I had to *time* it just right. And if I messed up or if I was wrong...boy! I'd be in big trouble.

Colossal trouble!

No time to think about that! Time to put the plan into motion.

Step one: Make the Tagger mad!

I found a picture of a chicken on the Internet. I imported it and started chopping it up. I put the chicken's head on Bubba's body. That would make the Tagger think I thought he *was* Bubba! I enlarged the chicken's feet. I pasted them where Bubba's shoes used to be. Now I had Bubba's body with a chicken's head and big ol' chicken feet!

It still needed something....

I enlarged the chicken's tail and pasted it onto Bubba's butt.

Ha ha! It looked bigger than ever!

And fluffy yellow!

Then I took a purple *Du-uh* talkie bubble from

one of the graffiti pictures and pasted it next to the Bubba-chicken's beak. And under the *Du-uh*, I added, *I'm the Tagger!*

I sat back and checked it over.

Looking good!

On my home page I built a link to the chicken page that said:

> **ATTENTION: TAGGER!**
> **I KNOW WHO YOU ARE,**
> **AND I WILL PROVE IT!**
> **(Click here for a clue.)**

I made another link called *Tagger Damage* that went to a page of graffiti pictures. It wasn't fancy or even that much—just a grid of pictures with labels—but at least it was a start.

I activated the updates.

It was time to spread the word!

Anybody that's ever written to shredderman@shredderman.com is in my Shredderman address book. By now I've got *hundreds* of e-mail addresses saved up!

And one golden one: bixby@bignet.com.

I get nasty e-mails from Bubba almost every morning. He hates that his butt is on the World

Wide Web, and I think he checks my site first thing every day.

But now this was good, because even if the Tagger didn't see the site on his own, Bubba would tell him all about it.

So I clicked on Compose and made a new e-mail that said TAGGER ALERT! in the subject line and typed:

You've seen his handiwork. On the Green Machine, on the hallowed walls of Old Town Square, on our historic Cedar Creek Bridge, even in the tube slides of a toddler park. The Tagger is hateful and harmful and (let's not mince words here) duuuu-uuuuh-dumb!

Do you want to see what this villain looks like?

Do you want to know him for what he is?

Then go to shredderman.com and click on the Attention: Tagger! *link. (Younger viewers, beware—it is not a pretty sight! Parental approval advised!)*

I laughed. That was sure to get kids clicking like crazy!

Next, I went to my address book, selected *all* the addresses, and sent them over to the Bcc box so everyone would get a copy but no one would know who else was getting copies.

I reread my letter. I spell-checked it. Then I set the priority to high so there'd be a bright red exclamation point when it arrived. I looked everything over again, held my breath, and clicked Send.

Just like that, copies flew through cyberspace!

To hundreds of different houses!

Boy, I love computers.

Just for fun, I went back to my site and checked it over. But then I noticed the little clock in the bottom right corner of my monitor.

3:45 A.M.?

How'd that happen?

I saved, shut down, and hopped into bed. And

the next morning, I staggered to school on less than three hours' sleep. No power-walking for me!

But the minute I was on campus, *boing*, I woke right up.

The police were there!

The Channel 12 news crew was there!

And from the graffiti on the wall, I knew the Tagger had already been to *shredderman.com*.

CHAPTER 11
Mistaken Identity

A giant purple dumb-baby was sprayed on the back wall of the library. But it didn't just say "Du-uh!" in the talkie bubble. It said, "I'm Shredderman! Du-uh!"

Kids were swarming all around, talking a hundred miles an hour. A lady with a Channel 12 microphone was spinning in circles trying to get interviews with third graders. "What do you think of all of this?" she asked a blond boy with bowl-cut hair.

The boy pulled a dumb-baby face right at the camera and said, "Du-uh!"

The Channel 12 lady rolled *her* eyes, then

waved her cameraman over to another little kid and tried again. "What do you think of this, uh, *Shredderman?*" she asked her.

"Shredderman?" the girl asked back. "Oh, Shredderman's *cool!*"

"Yeah! Totally cool!" another girl said.

The Channel 12 lady shook her head and sighed, then stuck her microphone in someone else's face.

I wanted to run up to the Channel 12 lady and say, "Wait! Shredderman didn't do the graffiti! The *Tagger* did!" But I couldn't. I couldn't say anything that would give me away.

The teachers were having some sort of powwow off to the side, and Dr. Voss was talking to a policeman. To Sergeant Klubb!

I moved closer. I tried to act invisible. Actually, I'm good at being invisible. At least that's what it feels like a lot. Like when we're picking teams. Or when people are talking about sleepovers. Or meeting at the park. Or going to the movies. . . . People don't seem to notice that I'm standing right there.

So I got real close to Dr. Voss and Sarge. And I was listening away when a hand clamped down on my shoulder. "Nolan!"

I jumped like a kangaroo. And when I landed, there was my dad, smiling down at me.

"I'm sorry, Nolan. Didn't mean to startle you!"

My heart was pounding at least 165 beats a minute. My eyelids were cranked back probably 190 degrees. My whole body went from 98.6 Fahrenheit to subzero Celsius like *that*.

Dad leaned down and whispered, "Take a deep breath, son. Take a deeeeeep breath."

I tried, but it's hard when your heart's racing and the rest of you is petrified.

He laughed. "You must've been concentrating on something pretty hard. Honestly, I wasn't trying to startle you . . . !"

Finally I blinked and said, "I...I...Uh, hi, Dad."

"Surprised to see me at school?"

"Uh-huh."

"Well, I got a call about the graffiti." He put his arm around my shoulders and moved us toward Sarge and Dr. Voss, looking at the graffiti the whole time. "Shredderman, huh?" He took a small spiral notebook from his coat pocket. "And all this time we've been calling him the Tagger."

"But he's not!" I cried. "I mean..."

He wasn't listening to me, anyway. He was shaking hands with Sergeant Klubb, saying, "Hey, Billy. Long time no see."

Sergeant Klubb snorted. "This punk's keeping us busy, huh?"

Dr. Voss looked mad. She had her arms crossed, and her lips were pulled tight. "And I suppose now you're going to accuse my *son* of doing this?"

"Look, Mrs. Voss—" Sarge said.

"*Doctor* Voss to you, Sergeant."

Sarge took a deep breath. "Ma'am, we never accused your son or the other boys we questioned of anything—we were simply looking for information."

"But the implication was clear!"

Sarge turned to my dad. "Tell her, Steven. Tell her about the tip."

Dad nodded and tried not to look at me. "It's true, Dr. Voss. An anonymous tip was left on my machine at the *Gazette*."

She huffed and said, "It was probably left by this . . . this *Shredderman*. He seems to think he can do whatever he wants, just like all delinquents."

Shredderman? A *delinquent*? How could they even *think* that? Shredderman fought for truth and justice! Shredderman was a *good* guy! Anyone who'd been to the site knew that!

Things had gone from bad to worse at light speed. And before I could figure out how to stop

something going 186,282 miles per second, Mrs. Bernhart, Miss Simms, and a bunch of other teachers started shooing kids off to class. "Didn't you hear the bell? Go! Go! Go! You'll all be tardy!"

My dad ruffled my hair and said, "Have a good day, Nolan! See you tonight."

Mr. Green caught up to me before I got in line

outside Room 22. "Nolan!" he whispered. "What were you *thinking*?"

"I didn't spray that!" I whispered back.

"I mean about the site. I got your e-mail this morning."

I shrugged. "I was trying to make him mad."

He laughed, but it wasn't a funny laugh. "Well, you did a good job! And he sure turned the tables on you!"

"I know! But how can people think that *Shredderman* did that?"

"People jump to conclusions, Nolan."

"Well, tell them he didn't do it!"

"Me?" He pointed to himself. "I can't tell them! I'm the Bouncer, remember?"

"But—"

"And the truth is, I'm feeling pretty uptight about all this. I'm not exactly Dr. Voss's favorite teacher to begin with, you know."

I didn't know. But now that he said it, it did

make sense. She was never very friendly to him, that's for sure. And she'd been pretty *mean* to him about his van.

Kids in line were starting to look around for him, so I said, "Don't worry, okay? I'll fix everything. I promise!"

He looked at me like my mom does when I tell her I know how to make my own lunch, then hurried to unlock the door.

CHAPTER 12
Mom and Dad Boot Up

By the time I got home from school, I felt weaker than a mortal. Forget superpowers—I was like Superman surrounded by kryptonite. What was I going to *do*?

Mom took one look at me and said, "Honey! What's wrong?"

I just sat down on the floor, backpack and all.

She felt my forehead. "Are you coming down with something?"

I shrugged, sighed, and lay down on the floor.

"Nolan!" She pulled me up. "Honey?"

"I'm okay, Mom," I finally said. "Just really tired." I was, too. Superhero or not, three hours' sleep is not enough.

She peeled off my shoes and dragged me to bed. "You get some sleep, young man." She felt my forehead again and said, "I'll check on you at dinnertime."

I must have snored through a time warp, because I swear she never left. One minute she's sitting on the edge of my bed, feeling my forehead, saying, "You get some sleep," and the next minute she's *still* on the edge of my bed, feeling my forehead, but now she's saying, "Honey? Honey, time to wake up."

The smell of dinner was floating through the air. "Spaghetti?" I asked.

"Lasagna."

I sat up. "Really?"

She laughed and said, "Feeling better?"

I swung out of bed. "Lots!"

"Good! You had me a little worried. And," she added, "your father is quite anxious to talk to you."

Uh-oh. I stopped in my tracks.

"About Shredderman," she said.

Uh-*double*-oh. "Shredderman?" I said as innocently as I could.

She shook her head. "Don't ask me—never heard of the guy before."

"Hi, Dad," I said when I sat down next to him at the table.

"Nolan! There you are!" He scooped a big square of lasagna onto his plate. "Your mom says you were wiped out when you got home from school."

"I'm okay now."

"Glad to hear it." He put some lasagna on my plate. "So, tell me—what do you know about Shredderman?"

I shrugged. "Not much."

"Hmmm." He served Mom. "Well, I'm getting conflicting reports. Some of the kids at your school told me he was trying to stop the Tagger. Other kids say he *is* the Tagger." He frowned. "Dr. Voss seems to think he's an all-around menace. A wolf in sheep's clothing."

"How come?"

"I don't know," he said. "She was in a pretty agitated state of mind when I tried to ask her about it—complained a lot about some Web site of his."

"A Web site?" My mouth was dry. My throat felt choked. What if they went to the site and could tell I had built it? What if they—

"She called it a cry for attention."

I almost jumped out of my chair and shouted, No way! It's a call for truth and justice! It's an awesome site! How can she not like it?

Then I remembered the link to **Bubba's Big Butt**.

Principals—and teachers and *parents*—are funny about butts.

And underwear.

And farts and burps and barf and B.O. and poop.

They make being an adult seem really, really boring.

"Nolan?"

"Huh?"

"Where were you just then?" my dad asked.

"I . . . I don't know. Daydreaming, I guess."

"Well, I was asking—what do *you* know about this Shredderman character?"

"Uh...that he's a good guy."

"A good guy who sprays graffiti?" my mom asked.

"He didn't spray it!" I cried.

"Oh?" they both said, looking at me.

Whoops.

I tried smiling. "At...at least I don't think he did. I think—"

The phone rang.

Phew.

Dad said, "Sorry, Eve, but I've got to get it. Just in case." We could hear him from over by Mom's desk. "Hello?...Hey, Sarge....Uh-huh...uh-huh....Seriously?...Uh-huh...uh-huh....Is that spelled just like it sounds?...Got it. Okay, I'll be sure to check it out."

"What was that about?" Mom asked after he hung up.

"Sarge went to that Web site—*shredderman.com*? Says it's a riot."

"So Shredderman's *not* the Tagger?" my mom asked.

"That's yet to be seen." He took a bite of lasagna. "But we'll get to the bottom of it."

After dinner, Dad booted up Mom's computer. He typed in *shredderman.com*.

Mom hung over his shoulder.

I held my breath.

All of a sudden, music blared from the speakers! Shredderman streaked across the top of the screen in his purple mask and cape! The SHREDDERMAN banner fluttered behind him! Then the Bouncer boinged into view. He flexed his tattooed muscles. One biceps popped up with TRUTH, the other popped up with JUSTICE.

My dad spotted the *Attention: Tagger!* link. He

clicked! And a few seconds later, he said, "Look at this, Eve! Shredderman's not the Tagger!"

My mom nodded. "But he's sure egging him on, don't you think? Calling him chicken and all?"

"Hmmm," my dad said. "But it does look like he meant well."

"Unless he's got a dark side." She glanced at my dad. "You know, like an alter ego?"

My dad laughed, "A schizophrenic superhero?"

"Steven, don't laugh! They're all a little that way when you think about it. Spider-Man, Superman, Batman...they're all tortured inside, don't you think?"

"Superman?" my dad asked. He was clicking on the *Jokes* link now. "How's Superman tortured? He's got superstrength, he's got X-ray vision, he can *fly*....Give me that kind of torture any day!"

"You're missing the whole point, Steven! He's tortured by his isolation. He's lonesome. They're all lonesome!"

"That doesn't mean they have a *dark* side. That just means—"

My mom cut him off. "You're telling me Batman doesn't have a dark side? You're telling me—"

"Oh, Eve, for cryin' out loud. They're *characters*. Somebody made them up! Whoever this Shredderman character is, he's *real*." He was scrolling through my *Jokes* page when suddenly he sat back and read, "'What do you call a bully fire?'"

My mom leaned forward and read the answer. "'A Bubba-que?'"

She looked at Dad.

Dad looked at her.

They both busted up.

Dad turned to me and said, "This has got to be about Alvin Bixby, don't you think? How many Bubbas can there be?"

I mumbled, "Looks like," and tried to breathe.

Mom looked at me. "Have you visited this site before?"

I shrugged. "I've *heard* about it."

"Well, with all the trouble Alvin's caused you—"

"Ha ha!" I laughed, pointing to a joke on the screen like I'd never seen it before. "'Why run from a bully? He's got the Bub-onic plague!'" I laughed again. "That's funny!"

Dad laughed, too, but Mom said, "But, Nolan, this site must belong to someone at your school—don't you think?"

I shrugged again. "I've heard some kids say they think it's one of the teachers."

Dad was clicking on the **What's big and fat and smells all over?** link.

I closed my eyes.

I held my breath.

He busted up. "Bubba's Big Butt? I don't think a *teacher* would have the nerve to put this on his Web site, do you?"

"No," Mom said. "It's got to be a student. A pretty funny one, too." She turned to me. "Do you know any sixth graders who are really good at computers?"

I tried to look innocent. "A lot of kids have their own Web site."

Dad snapped his fingers. "Hey! I'll bet Sarge can find out who this site is registered to."

"Good idea," Mom said.

Uh-triple-oh!

I escaped to my room and just sat on my bed, trying to catch my breath.

How long would it be before Mom and Dad found out who *shredderman.com* was registered to?

And what would happen to me when they found out it was registered to *them*?

CHAPTER 13
Dirty Disguise

Shredderman.com wasn't actually registered to my mom and dad. It was registered to Shredderman. But Shredderman had used Eve Byrd's credit card number. And even though I'd taken all the privacy options, I didn't know how much information a reporter like my dad—or a police friend like Sarge—could dig up.

If Shredderman was going to catch the Tagger, I had to act fast. The first part of my plan had backfired, and now that a lot of people thought Shredderman *was* the Tagger, I didn't have much to lose.

But to pull off the rest of my plan, I was going

to need bionic hearing *and* X-ray vision *and* an invisibility cloak.

Or I was going to have to ditch school.

Ditch school?

I'd never even thought such a thought!

But boy oh boy, I was thinking it now.

It was the only way.

I had a lot to do before morning, though. A lot!

First step—write an e-mail. One that I'd send to only one address.

Bixby@bignet.com.

I couldn't send it to everyone—that would blow everything! And since I didn't know the Tagger's e-mail address, the next best thing was Bubba's. He would tell the Tagger. He had to!

I got to work on my message. It had to be just right!

So I wrote it.

And rewrote it.

And rewrote it again!

And when I was all done, I sat back and read it.

The Tagger's not cool. He's not sly. He's not funny. He's not smart.

What he is, is a coward. Totally chicken. If he wasn't chicken, he'd do something real. Something dangerous. Anyone can tag the side of a building. Big deal. Anyone can spray the inside of a kiddie slide. Whoop-de-do! But here's something the Tagger would never spray:

Ivana Voss's car.

Why? Because that would take guts. Brawk-brawk-brawk, Tagger! You're lame!

Would the Tagger take the bait? If it was Ryan, would he really spray-paint his own mother's car? He'd know it was a trap, but with Bubba and his friends teasing him about the challenge, he'd be pressured into it.

At least that's what I was counting on!

I saved the e-mail to my draft folder—I couldn't send it yet! Timing was everything! Then I did my homework and went to bed. And even though it was late, I wasn't sleepy. Not one bit! I just lay there in bed, running my plan through my head over and over again.

When I was sure Mom and Dad were finally asleep, I got up.

I pulled dark sweats over my pajamas.

I put my safety scissors in a sweatshirt pocket and wiggled into my shoes.

Then I did something I'd never done before—I opened my window, pulled out the screen, climbed through, and jumped.

The ground was only about a four-foot drop, but for a second there it felt like I was flying. I landed like a real superhero, too—feet steady, hands out.

Oh, yeah!

I skulked across the street, looking all around. I was smooth. I was quick. The streetlights were bright, but I don't think anyone saw me.

I was in sneak mode!

Instead of using the sidewalk, I went down to the soccer field. Then I crept up to the teachers' parking lot through the bushes. Not a car any-where, but aha! The yard-waste bags were still piled up by the office.

I swooped down on them without a sound. Lots were heavy with grass clippings, but I found one full of big dry leaves that was light.

Voom! I threw it over my shoulder.

Tip-tip-tip-tip-tip-tip-tip! I tiptoed across the parking lot. The bag was full, but carrying it was easy!

I felt like some sort of Super-Santa!

I moved it into the bushes. I untied the bag's drawstrings. I emptied half of the leaves.

I had to make room for me!

A totally empty sack would have been easier, and for sure more comfortable. But I wasn't doing this for ease or comfort.

I was doing this to catch a villain!

Plus, a boy in a sack does not look like yard waste. It looks like a boy in a sack.

When I was done dumping leaves, I started

cutting flaps. Flaps that hinged on top. Two on the bottom for the legs, two on the sides for the arms, one in front for the face, and inside the face flap, another little three-inch flap for my right eye.

My camera eye.

Then I hauled my trash sack disguise back up the hill. I lost a few leaves out of the flaps along the way, but not too bad! I hid my sack behind the other yard-waste sacks and looked all around. Had anybody seen me?

No. The whole block looked deserted. I crouched by the sacks for a minute just to be sure. It felt weird being at school alone. In the dark. I felt like I'd been beamed up to a distant planet in the galaxy.

Only there was my house, right across the street.

When I left the sack and ran for home, it felt like I was running under negative G's. I was weightless! Across the parking lot. Across the street! I was flying!

Gravity started working again when I tried to get back in the window. Boy! It took me forever!

When I finally got inside, I put my screen back in, set my alarm, and hit the hay.

My brain was zooming with doubts. Timing was everything, but how long should I wait? I couldn't send the e-mail too soon— Ryan would have the chance to tag his mother's car in their own driveway!

But what if Bubba didn't check his computer before school? What if he didn't call Ryan in time? I'd be ditching school for nothing!

But the more I thought about it, the more I convinced myself that my plan would work. I'd gotten same-day action with my TAGGER

ALERT! e-mail...and they were probably now on *red* alert.

Plus, Ryan would be more of a big shot to his friends if he tagged his mother's car at school. And it would be easier to cover his tracks. There'd be hundreds of kids to question! Lots of suspects.

But was I really going to ditch school? Was I really going to hide in a trash sack? Was I really going to...

When my alarm buzzed in the morning, I felt like I hadn't slept a wink. But there was no time to snooze!

I jumped out of bed.

I booted up my computer.

I read the e-mail over one last time.

Then I clicked on Send and crossed my fingers that my plan wouldn't backfire again.

CHAPTER 14
Trash Sack Hero

The minute the message was gone, my heart started pumping. There was no going back now! I was either going to be a hero or in some hot water. I'm talking 100 degrees Celsius.

212 Fahrenheit!

Boiling hot!

I dove back into bed. Too late to worry about that now. I had work to do!

Next step: act sick so Mom would believe me later when I told her I came home sick from school.

I started coughing. *Cough-cough-cough*. Not too hard. Not too soft. *Cough-cough-cough*.

I waited a minute. Nobody came.

I tried a little louder—*cough-cough-cough*—
and moaned a little for good measure.

Nobody came.

So, *cough-cough-cough* I went again. *Louder*.

This time there was a *tap-tap-tap* on my door.
"Honey?" my mom said, sticking her head inside.
"Are you okay?"

I sat up and nodded, then held my head like it
hurt.

"Are you sure?" She sat next to me and felt my
forehead.

I nodded again but moved my eyes from one
side to the other like Dad always does when he's
checking to see if he's got the flu. Then I coughed
some more—*cough-cough-cough*.

Mom hurried out of the room and was back a
minute later with the ear-scope thermometer.
She pulled up the top of my ear and jabbed the
thermometer down the canal.

A perfect 98.6 degrees Fahrenheit, 37 degrees Celsius.

She jabbed it down my other ear.

Same thing.

"I'm fine, Mom." *Cough-cough-cough*.

"If you're not, I can arrange to work from home today...."

Uh-oh. I was laying it on too thick. "I'm okay. Really."

I burned the toast at breakfast just to prove it. And after I'd cleared the dishes, I went down to my room, put on my army pants, and stashed my digital camera and my safety scissors in one of the cargo pockets. Then I headed back to the kitchen to load up my other pockets.

Juice boxes—check!

Granola bars—check!

Big straws—check!

Pack of gum—check!

Rubber bands—check!

Dad had left for work early, so I called, "Bye, Mom!" and headed for the door.

She blocked my way, saying, "All right, this is *proof* something's wrong."

"Huh?"

She crossed her arms and looked me up and down. "What *is* going on with you, Nolan?"

"Huh?" I said again, and tried hard not to look down at my cargo pockets. Were they bulging way out? Were they *leaking*?

She squinted at me. "You hate that shirt."

I looked from one arm to the other. I did hate it. It was long-sleeved and muddy green and it had a pointy collar and an itchy tag. But it was perfect for what I had to do.

She squinted harder. "And it really does not go with those pants—which you know *I* hate."

"Mom, I love these pants! They're...they're cool."

Her face crinkled. "Cool? Nolan, have you *looked* at yourself?"

"Mo-om! First you complain that I won't wear this shirt; now you're complaining that I am! Can I please just go to school?"

She shook her head, but finally she sighed and said, "Go." But then she noticed the clock. "Wait! What am I saying? It's way too early for you to go to school!"

"I know, but I promised Mr. Green I'd help him with a project before school."

She waved her hand through the air. "Okay, okay! Go!"

I started trucking for the door, but before I could reach it, she cried, "Wait!" *again.*

I whipped around. "*What*, Mom!" Wow. I sounded mean. But I was running out of time!

She raised an eyebrow. "Your backpack?" she said, watching me carefully. "Don't you want your backpack?"

"Oh. Oh, right." I strapped it on while she felt my forehead and muttered something about my "erratic behavior."

When I finally got away from her, I ditched my backpack in some bushes near the garage and zoomed across the street.

There were already cars in the parking lot, including a fancy silver one with spoked wheels.

Dr. Voss's!

I hid in the bushes in my muddy green itchy-tagged shirt and army pants. When the coast was clear, I zoomed across the parking lot. I ducked behind the stack of yard-waste sacks. And I was just starting to open my disguise sack when a yellow Volkswagen drove into the parking lot.

I waited.

Mrs. Bernhart got out.

Then a black SUV drove into the lot.

Drat!

I waited.

Miss Simms climbed out.

"Hi, Peggy!" "Good morning, Liza!" they called

to each other. Then they just *stood* there yakking away.

Double drat! How long were they going to stand around talking? I couldn't wait forever! I stayed low and untied my yard-waste sack. I stuck my right foot inside and through a bottom flap. I pushed my left foot in. My heart was racing like crazy! My eyes were boinging from the sack to the yakky teachers. I wiggled my body through the leaves and pulled the sack up around me.

No going back now!

Then the Green Machine turned into the parking lot, its motor making a real cool *boop-boop-boop-boop-boop* sound. Dumb-Baby was still all over the dolphins and it looked worse than ever.

Stupid Tagger.

The van backfired a little when Mr. Green turned off the motor, and I noticed Mrs. Bernhart and Miss Simms pull faces at it before they hurried away.

Just like popular kids do when they see *me* coming.

Wow, I thought. They're acting like they don't like Mr. Green! How could anyone not like Mr. Green? He was nice, and smart, and funny. Mr. Green was cool!

I wanted to say, "Pssssst!" and wave him over, but I didn't. Another car was coming into the parking lot, and besides, I didn't have time to talk to my sidekick. I had to hide!

I stayed on my knees and got all the way inside the sack. I stuck my arms out. I pulled the drawstrings tight over my head and tied them! I pulled my arms back in and held real still.

Nobody came and said, Hey! Whatcha doing? so after a minute, I started to feel safe.

I'd done it!

I was completely disguised!

And boy! Was my disguise dark. And stuffy!

I pulled in the face flap and took a few deep breaths while I looked around. More cars were coming in. I had to get going!

I dug up the pack of gum and put two pieces in my mouth, chewing like crazy. When the gum was soft, I pinched off part of it and used it to hold open the eye flap. Then I cut the straws in half, looped them together with a rubber band, and stuck one end in my mouth and the other out the flap. I breathed in. Ah! Fresh air! My very own trash sack snorkel!

Okay. I could see, I could breathe....It was time to get my camera ready!

There was enough light coming in through the eye flap for me to see what I was doing. And once I had the camera ready, I stood halfway up and tiptoed around the other yard-waste sacks. Hee hee hee! I felt like I was in a Bugs Bunny cartoon!

I got as close to Dr. Voss's car as I could, then squatted so my feet didn't show and waited.

More cars came in. The buses drove up and dropped kids off in front of the school. Pretty soon there were people everywhere, walking all around me. One kid even jumped *over* me! I could see everyone, but no one noticed me.

It was the perfect disguise!

Then the tardy bell rang and after a few minutes it was quiet. Completely quiet.

I stayed as still as I could for as long as I could. But my legs were stiff from squatting, and I finally had to shift around and sit down.

Then I waited some more. The tag on my shirt was itchy, but the leaves poking me everywhere were even itchier. And it was getting hard to keep my lips tight around my snorkel. And what *was* that smell? The warmer it got, the stronger it got. Was there...was there dog poop somewhere in these leaves?

I tried to forget about it. But thinking I was stuck in a sack with dog poop was grossing me out!

Then the sun started beating down on my sack and pretty soon I felt like I was cooking inside it. I was sweating, I was itchy, and the smell was getting worse and worse.

I pulled in my snorkel and drank a juice. What

kind of stupid idea was this? What kind of super-hero hides in a poopy trash sack sucking down juice boxes? I needed air. *Lots* of air!

I was about to break down and tack the whole face flap open with a piece of gum when I heard a sound.

Was it footsteps?

Yes! Quick footsteps! *Sneaky* footsteps! Coming from behind me!

I held my breath.

The footsteps got closer.

And closer.

And *closer*.

Then they stopped, right behind me!

Something bumped me, hard. And for a minute I thought I was busted. But then there he was, crawling around me, heading straight for Dr. Voss's car!

The Tagger!

I put my camera up and zoomed in on him.

He checked over both shoulders.

He sneaked open the back door.

He pulled out a spray can!

And then he did it—Ryan Voss sprayed a dumb-baby face on his own mother's car.

CHAPTER 15
Up, Up, and Away!

I got a movie clip of the whole thing. And I almost busted out of my disguise and cried, "Gotcha, you villain!"

Good thing Ryan didn't give me the chance. Revealing my secret identity by popping out of a stinky sack wouldn't exactly help Shredderman's image.

Not to mention my already poopy image as Nolan Byrd.

In the blink of an eye, Ryan had slipped the spray can back inside the car—probably under the seat, where Dr. Voss would never think to look—and was *gone*.

But still. I was bursting with excitement. I'd

trapped him! I'd really trapped him! I zoomed back through the movie clip and viewed it from the beginning. Yes! There he was, spraying his own mom's car! Yes, yes, yes! I about boinged up and down in my yard-waste sack.

I checked out my face flap window.

Nobody to the right...

Nobody to the left...

But uh-oh. A truck was slowing down.... It was turning into the parking lot.... It was a *gardener's* truck. One with rakes and hoes. One half full of...uh-double-oh! Yard-waste sacks!

I had to get out of my disguise! Fast! Only just then someone *screamed*. It wasn't a little *eeeek,* either.

It was loud!

It was shrill!

It was *close.*

I turned sideways and peeked out my right armhole.

It was Dr. Voss!

She circled her car, screaming, crying, yelling for Mrs. Holler to call the police. And boy! Who'd ever guess a principal knew so many four-letter words!

I stowed my camera safely inside a cargo pocket,

then shriveled up and inched back as much as I could. What would Dr. Voss do if she found me? Oh, no! She'd probably think *I* was the Tagger! I had proof I wasn't, but what if she got mad and threw my camera? What if she destroyed my evidence?

Pretty soon the place was swarming with adults. They were everywhere! I was going from flap to flap, trying to figure out what to do! I needed more air! I needed to get *out* of there! I needed...uh-oh...the

gardener was backing his truck right over the curb. Right up to the sacks!

The driver got out.

His partner got out.

They dropped the tailgate, hiked up their pants, and started flinging sacks into the truck.

Uh-quintuple-oh!

I peeked out the front flap. Dr. Voss was still stomping around! I looked out the side flap. Those gardeners would be at me in no time! I was 76 pounds! 34.5 kilograms! They'd break their backs!

They didn't break their backs. They just hurled me on top and went back for more.

I didn't break mine, either, getting tossed in, but boy! when two other sacks landed on me, I was squished! I was dying for air!

I was afraid to shove my arms out yet, but believe me, I pried open the face hole so I could breathe! And that's when I saw the police cars pulling up to the school.

The gardeners got in the truck quick and bumped off the curb and onto the street. I watched the school get smaller. And smaller. And then the truck zoomed around the corner and the school disappeared.

I didn't know where we were going, but we were sure going there fast!

I had to get off the truck!

I tried untying the sack. I couldn't see what I was doing! I couldn't get it open!

I tried ripping the plastic. It was really strong!

So I got my scissors and *cut* myself out. Just rip, snip, snip, like I was coming out of some stinky, sweaty cocoon.

I stayed low, hiding under other sacks so the gardeners wouldn't see me in the rearview mirror. And I was planning to climb out at the first red light, only we kept hitting *green* lights. And forget stop signs! They treated them like *slow* signs.

Pretty soon I wouldn't know where I was!

I had to do *some*thing.

So I pushed off the sack I was hiding under. I flipped around. I stuck my thumbs in my ears, pressed my face up to the cab window, and shouted, "Wroooagggh!"

The driver smashed on the brakes—which pushed my face into the window even harder—

but when we stopped, I charged for the tailgate, swung myself over, and *ran*.

I was never so happy to get home in my whole life. It took me at least an hour. Maybe two! What kept me going was the movie clip. I watched it about twenty times. I couldn't *wait* to get it on the Internet!

After I got my backpack out of the bushes, I snuck through the garage door, dug the house key out of the nail can, and let myself in. Then I went to the laundry room, emptied all my pockets, and stripped down to my underwear.

Maybe most superheroes know how to do their own laundry, but this one didn't. But I couldn't exactly

leave my clothes in the laundry basket—they
were suspiciously dusty and dirty. And if clothes
can breathe, well, mine had bionic breath.
Pee-yew!

So I read the knobs on the washer, measured
out some soap, and got the machine running.

Hey...piece of cake!

I raced down to the bathroom, took the speediest shower ever, zoomed to my room, and booted up my computer. It was payback time!

I loaded the movie clip.

Beau-ti-ful!

I made a *Tagger in Action* link that took you straight to it.

Wa-hoo-hoo!

I linked the other images I'd gotten at Old Town Square—which I could finally use—and made a *Tagger's Dumb-Baby Friends* link on my home page. *Who else knew who the Tagger was?* it said above it. *Click here to see!* And under the images I'd gotten at Old Town, I lined up the yearbook mugshots I had scanned in and typed in their names below them: *Alvin "Bubba" Bixby, Ryan "Tagger" Voss, Carl Blanco, Manny Davis,* and *A. J. Penne.*

I ran to the laundry room. The washer was done! I threw my clothes in the dryer.

Cranked the knob to High.

Pushed the On button.

Around they went, *rrruhr-rrruhr-rrruhr!*

Laundry's easy!

I raced back down to my room. There was still one more thing I wanted to do, but I was having an intergalactic war in my head over it.

It was a little bit mean.

But then, this person had been a little bit mean to my sidekick. Actually, really mean. And buster, I don't care who you are, you don't mess with my sidekick!

So I scanned in an image of Dr. Voss from my yearbook. Then I made an *I'm the Tagger's Mother!* link that took you to her picture and said: *I'm Doctor Ivana Voss, the principal at Cedar Valley Elementary. My phone number is 714-555-9853. Isn't my son wonderful? Please call and let me know what you think.*

I was having a blast!

The phone rang. And even though it was down

the hall by my mom's desk, it shot me out of my seat.

After four rings, the recorder picked up. "You've reached Eve 'n' Steven's. Please leave a message at the beep." *Beeeeeep*. Then came my mother's voice, "Nolan? Honey, if you can hear this, pick up the phone!"

"Hello...?" I said, like my nose was stuffed with snot.

"Nolan!"

"Hi, Mom."

"'Hi, Mom'? I can't believe this! What are you doing home?"

"I came home sick, Mom," I said through my nose.

"Why didn't the school know that?"

"Because I...I just left."

"You didn't check out?"

"Nuh-uh. I didn't want you to have to come home."

"Nolan!"

"Mom, I told you—I can take care of myself."

"But—"

"Everything's fine, Mom. I haven't burned down the house or anything. Now I'm going to go back to bed, okay?"

"Nolan—"

"Please, Mom? I really want to lie down."

"I'll be right there."

"No! I mean, I'm okay. Really!"

"I'm coming home," she said, and hung up.

I yanked my clothes out of the dryer. They were hot! I raced down to my room, updated my site, sent an Extra, Extra, See All About It! Tagger Snagged! e-mail to everyone in the Shredderman address book, then shut down my computer and hopped into bed.

A few minutes later, my mom was home.

Then—uh-oh—my dad came slamming through the door.

And I could tell from the look on their faces that I'd jumped out of the poop sack and into deep doo-doo.

CHAPTER 16
Busted!

My mom stood by my bed with her arms crossed. My dad sat in my desk chair, studying me. He started to say something, but my mom put out a hand and said, "Let me, Steven."

Dad nodded.

I coughed. *Cough-cough-cough.*

"Do you know *why* I called here?" Before I could answer, she said, "I called here because Mrs. Holler phoned me at work. She wanted to know why you were absent today."

Mrs. Holler did that when you were absent? I had no idea! I said, "I'm sorry, Mom. I guess I should have called you. But I didn't want you to have to come home. I'm not throwing up or anything." *Cough-cough-cough.*

"She said you hadn't been at school all day."

I shrugged.

Dad leaned in a little and said, "So you came home during morning recess?"

I looked from my mom to my dad and back again. Then I said through my nose like I had a monster cold, "I'm sorry, okay? I should have told you!"

My dad said, "Nolan, look at me."

I looked at him, but it was hard.

"My question to you, son, is why didn't I see you when I came home at around eleven o'clock?"

Uh-oh.

"Where *were* you at eleven o'clock?"

My mouth opened and closed like a stupid fish.

"No... I don't believe it!" my mom cried. "Please tell me it isn't you...!"

"Who isn't me?" I choked out.

"The Tagger!"

I sat straight up. "The *Tagger*? You think *I'm* the Tagger?"

My mom was pacing all over my room, throwing her hands up in the air, crying. "The school called the parents of *all* children who were absent today, trying to figure out who spray-painted Dr. Voss's car."

"It wasn't me, Mom! I swear it wasn't me!"

The phone rang.

"Then why can't you tell us where you were at eleven o'clock? Your father stopped by the house, got a soda and a snack, used the bathroom.... He says your door was wide open. Did he just not *see* you? I don't think so! Nolan, you've been acting so *strangely* lately. Is this... is this why?"

"No! No, it's not!" I shouted.

I guess I forgot to talk through my nose, because all of a sudden her face squeezed together. "You're

not sick at all, are you?" She pulled away from me and wailed, "Oh, Nolan!"

I couldn't *believe* she thought I was the Tagger. And maybe superheroes aren't supposed to cry, but this one did. And once I started, I couldn't seem to stop. My breathing got all mixed up, and pretty soon I had the stupid hiccups.

We could hear the answering machine pick up. "You've reached Eve 'n' Steven's. Please leave a message at the beep." *Beeeeeep*. Dad perked an ear as a voice said, "Steven, this is Sarge—"

Dad got up and whispered, "I'll be right back."

Mom sat on the edge of my bed and said, "Nolan? Nolan, please talk to me. You've always been an honest child. Now please, tell me the truth."

I just buried my head under my pillow. How could they think I was the Tagger? It was bad enough that they thought I couldn't *do* anything. But how could they think I was a villain?

I was the good guy!

I was about to choke to death on hiccups when I heard my dad saying, "Sarge says Shredderman's posted a movie clip. He says it exposes the Tagger."

"Oh, no!" my mom wailed.

I said, "I'm not—*hic*—the—*hic*—Tagger!" Then I sat up and said it louder, "I'm not—*hic*—the—*hic*—Tagger!"

Dad was already booting up my computer. Mom got up and stood behind him.

I just sat there, hiccuping.

When they saw the clip, my dad's jaw dropped.

My mom gasped, "Ryan *Voss*? And he sprayed his own mother's car?"

My dad leaned back and rubbed his chin. "Well, I'll be."

They both turned to face me. "So...so you're really not the Tagger?" Mom asked.

I scowled at her and hiccuped. "Of course not!"

"But...but then where *were* you at eleven o'clock? Why did you leave school?"

Hic.

Slowly my dad's forehead crept back. His jaw eased open. His eyes bulged.

Hic.

He scoured my desk and spotted my yearbook sticking out of my scanner. He yanked it out and saw Dr. Voss's face. "You're..." He was blinking like crazy at me. "You're..." He snatched up my digital camera and found the movie clip. Then he looked at my mother and whispered, "Eve, our son is...a superhero!"

"What?"

"Look!" He showed her the clip. "He's not the Tagger, he's Shredderman!"

"*What?*" she said again, and now *she* was blinking like crazy.

"Shredderman!" my dad said with a grin. "Definitely the coolest superhero to hit this town!"

My mom covered her mouth. "*You* built that site? All by yourself?"

I nodded. *Hic.*

"But *how*? How did you know how to do...all of this?" She was back at the computer, clicking around like mad. "This is amazing! Look at this graphic! Honey, I program computers, and I don't know how to do half of this stuff!" She turned to face me. "Where did you...how did you...?"

I shrugged. "It's not hard."

"Ha!" she laughed.

Dad scooted way close to me. "Nolan, you've got to tell me how you managed to get that clip of Ryan Voss tagging his mother's car. How in the world did you *do* that?"

So I told him all about it. Every detail, clear through my getaway in the gardener's truck. And while my dad was grinning bigger and bigger, my mom's face was turning whiter and whiter.

"You...you jumped out up by Route 7?" she gasped.

"Uh-huh." The hiccups were gone.

"That's *miles* away! You could've gotten lost! Or been kidnapped! What if you'd been hit by a car? What if—"

"Mo-om! Superheroes don't get lost or kidnapped. Well, if they do get kidnapped, they always find a way out of it, right? I'm fine!"

"But...you could've suffocated!"

"I had air holes! A snorkel! I'm fine! And don't worry—I took a shower. And washed my clothes."

She checked me over. "In the washer and dryer?"

"No," I said, rolling my eyes, "in the shower."

"In the *shower?*"

Dad said, "He's kidding, Eve. You know, a joke?"

"Yeah," I said. "Maybe someday I'll even figure out how to toast waffles."

She looked at me, blinking away. Then she
threw her arms around me and started bawling.
"My baby!"

"Mo-om!" I rolled my eyes at my dad.

He grinned and winked at me.

So I hugged her back, and the truth is, I was
glad they'd found out.

Super glad.

CHAPTER 17
Truth and Justice Prevail!

Even though I went back to the beginning and told them everything, Mom and Dad still had questions the next morning. I didn't mind answering them, though. It was like we were all in a secret club together.

I liked it.

My dad covered for me with the school. He told Mrs. Holler that I'd been with him the whole time.

The school didn't even seem to care. I guess they were too embarrassed that the town tagger was the principal's son.

The story was all over the news. Channel 12 showed Ryan being stuffed in the back of Sarge's car, and the news lady tried to get Dr. Voss to say something, but she just ducked under her arm and ran away.

My dad wrote a big piece on it, too. Said it would seem suspicious if he didn't. His headline was SHREDDERMAN SAVES CEDAR VALLEY. I told

him it sounded corny, but he did it anyway. "Why not?" he said. "Not every town can boast its own superhero!"

"But what if people try to find out who Shredderman is?"

Dad grinned. "Didn't I tell you? That's my new assignment." He tisked and shook his head. "And I have a hunch he's going to be one tough superhero to unmask."

The next day, everyone was talking about what a jerk Ryan Voss was and how it served him right that he was going to have to spend his weekends painting walls and cleaning gum off sidewalks.

Everyone but Bubba. Bubba kept muttering about what a jerk Shredderman was and how someday he was gonna get him.

We'll see about that!

We also found out that Dr. Voss is going to pay for a new mural for the Green Machine. Mr. Green says he probably won't have dolphins again—that it just wouldn't be the same. He told the class he was thinking about trolls.

"Trolls?" Miriam Wipple asked him. "Those ugly overgrown elves with sharp teeth and dirty fingernails?"

"Friendly trolls," he told her. "In a forest scene with ferns and trees and oversized mushrooms. Or maybe I'll paint the whole van dark blue and have a comet streaking across the sky."

"Cool!" everyone said, so I think maybe he'll go with the comet.

Mom and Dad were very interested in hearing about the van. They used to kind of say, Uh-huh, uh-huh, whenever I talked about Mr. Green, but now that they know he's the Bouncer, they really sit up and listen. Especially since the four of us had a powwow about Shredderman and the site and what we should do to keep it a secret.

Mr. Green said, "We have to keep a lid on it, or I'll need to look for a new job."

"Why?" I asked him. "They can't fire you for being my sidekick!"

My dad said, "That's right! You haven't done anything illegal or even wrong."

Mr. Green shook his head. "Dr. Voss was pretty fried over the way you exposed her son." He chuckled. "And that little link to her? Oh, she was fit to be tied."

"But I already took her phone number off the site! Mom made me."

"Yeah, but before you did, she got calls from all over. I heard a woman from Australia called to scold her!"

From Australia? That was halfway around the world!

"Really?" my mom said.

"Cool!" my dad said.

Mr. Green flexed an arm. "Here's to truth!"

We all put our arms up and pumped. "And justice!"

I went to bed that night feeling great. The Shredderman site counter was up to ten thousand! Ten thousand visitors! Sure, all I'd really done with the site was collar a bully and trap a tagger, but inside it felt . . . bigger than that. Inside it felt like there was still more to do.

Maybe the way I was searching for truth and justice had started out small, but I could feel it growing. Spreading. From my little bedroom, through my school, and now my town!

So maybe I can't fly through the air like Superman, but my *ideas* can fly across a web bigger than anything even *Spider-Man* could make—the World Wide Web!

So whatever's next, in the name of truth and justice, I'll be there!